AVIARY SCHOOL

CUENTO
DE LUZ

To my mother, whose delicious stews never failed to cheer me up.

Clucky and the Magic Kettle

Text © 2012 Mar Pavón
Illustrations © 2012 Mónica Carretero
This edition © 2012 Cuento de Luz SL
Calle Claveles 10 | Urb Monteclaro | Pozuelo de Alarcón | 28223 Madrid | Spain
www.cuentodeluz.com
Original title in Spanish: Cocorina y el puchero mágico
English translation by Jon Brokenbrow
ISBN: 978-84-15619-44-4
Printed by Shanghai Chenxi Printing Co., Ltd. in PRC, August 2012, print number 1305-03

FSC
www.fsc.org
MIX
Paper from
responsible sources
FSC® C007923

Clucky and the Magic Kettle

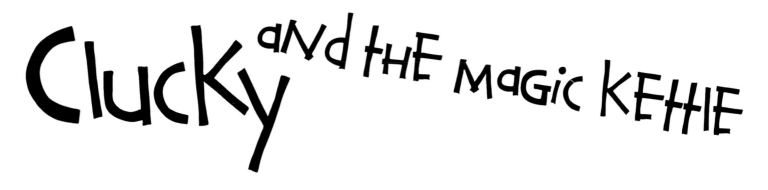

Mar Pavón

illustrated by Mónica Carretero

Clucky the Hen takes
her kids, as a rule,
To learn and have fun
at the barnyard school.

Hide-and-go-seek
is their favorite game,
At recess they play
it again and again.

But then Mr. Goose set
their hearts all a-flurry,
With something he said that
made the chicks worry:
"Your mom's memory's weak,
you know this is true,
One day she could leave
and forget about you!"

The chicks asked their mom
at the end of the day,
"Could you ever forget us?"
She answered, "No way!"
"I love you my darlings,"
the mother hen said,
"What nonsense is this?
Get that out of your head!"

Every day you can see
how Clucky, with pride,
Takes her chicks into
school on a tricycle ride.

They learn how to read,
and so many things!
They paint and they draw,
and they learn how to sing.

But then peacock chick
got them thinking again,
With something he said
about one of their friends:
"Stay clear of that duckling,
his beak twists in song!
It could happen to you,
if you three tag along."

Once again after school,
they asked their mom, Clucky,
"Will we get twisted beaks
if we hang out with Ducky?"
"Don't be silly my dears,"
the mother hen said,
"What nonsense is this?
Get that out of your head!"

So still you can see
our famous hen mother
Take her chicks into school
one day after another.
They go to their gym class
where they exercise tummies
To learn to lay eggs
and become loving mummies.

But this time the pigeon
and his little bunch
Made fun of the chicks
when they went out to lunch.
"You know why you fools
    are the talk of the town?
        You're nothing like us,
            you were hatched upside down!"

So that afternoon,
they asked Clucky with fright,
"Is it true we are dumb
because you can't lay eggs right?"
"How can you believe
what that pigeon said?
What nonsense is this?
Get that out of your head!"

AVIARY SCHOOL

In the quiet of night,
from her kitchen comes a smell.
With her kettle on the boil,
Clucky brews her magic spell.

Into the pot go spite and envy,
in go nasty feelings, too,
Plus a little shake of stardust
to add some magic to her brew.

"Hubble bubble boil and bubble,
hubble bubble boil and brew.
Hubble bubble toil and trouble,
hubble bubble boil and stew."

She boils the potion down for hours,
letting out a weary cluck.
She pours it out into a jar,
and adds a label reading "yuk!!"

"Reduce, reuse, recycle!"
Clucky likes to say.
Envy turns to admiration,
nasty feelings go away.
Spite turns into love for others,
with support and gratitude.
With respect for those around us,
it's time to change our attitude!

Clucky the Hen takes
her chicks every day
To their aviary school,
where they all learn and play.

There they are happy,
they make friends who care,
Friends who are loving,
who listen and share.

Now all would be lovely,

all would be fine,

If Clucky could just get them all to school on time!

Mar Pavón (Barcelona 1968)

Wings have played a very important role in Mar Pavón's life: the stories she heard as a child allowed her imagination to sprout wings; a pencil and sheet of paper were the perfect wings for her fantasies to start to take shape; and years later, the births of her children gave her the ideal wings to soar into the world of story books, where one Spring day in 2010 she discovered Clucky, with all of her faults, virtues, and of course her wings, covered with the softest, downiest feathers. She is also the author of "Could It Happen To Anyone?" and "Zaira and the Dolphins," tales that allow children's imaginations to soar into the sky just like her own. And that, without doubt, is the first step towards HAPPINESS.

Mónica Carretero (Madrid 1971)

With an imagination like something out of a Marx Brothers movie, Mónica never stops drawing characters and inventing stories that leap out of her head and into her books. Characters who are full of life, color and tenderness, with hugs and kisses all around (maybe you have to look closely to find them, but they're always there!). And of course, there's always a piece of stripy clothing. Mónica has illustrated dozens of books, and has won awards in London and the USA.